The Snowy Special

Based on *The Railway Series* by the Rev. W. Awdry

Illustrations by
Robin Davies

EGMONT

EGMONT

We bring stories to life

First published in Great Britain 2008
by Egmont UK Limited
239 Kensington High Street, London W8 6SA

Thomas the Tank Engine & Friends™

CREATED BY BRITT ALLCROFT

Based on the Railway Series by the Reverend W Awdry
© 2008 Gullane (Thomas) LLC. A HIT Entertainment company.
Thomas the Tank Engine & Friends and Thomas & Friends are trademarks of Gullane (Thomas) Limited.
Thomas the Tank Engine & Friends and Design is Reg. U.S. Pat. & Tm. Off.

HiT entertainment

ISBN 978 1 4052 4088 8
5 7 9 10 8 6 4
Printed in Italy

FSC

Mixed Sources

Product group from well-managed
forests and other controlled sources

Cert no. TT-COC-002332
www.fsc.org
© 1996 Forest Stewardship Council

Egmont is passionate about helping to preserve the world's remaining ancient forests.
We only use paper from legal and sustainable forest sources.

This book is made from paper certified by the Forestry Stewardship Council (FSC),
an organisation dedicated to promoting responsible management of forest resources.
For more information on the FSC, please visit www.fsc.org. To learn more about
Egmont's sustainable paper policy, please visit www.egmont.co.uk/ethical

TO THE TRAINS ➡

This is a story about Henry, who, one snowy day, thought he couldn't manage without his lucky trucks. But as you and I both know, Really Useful Engines don't need trucks to be lucky ...

Winter had arrived on Sodor, and a thick blanket of snow covered the Island.

Snowdrifts blocked many of the lines and the tracks were very slippery.

The engines felt frozen from their funnels to their footplates.

But Henry the Green Engine puffed happily through the snowy countryside.

None of *his* lines were blocked!

That evening, Henry met Thomas in Tidmouth sheds.

"You are the only engine to have made your deliveries on time today," chuffed Thomas. "You must have lucky trucks!"

Henry saw that none of the other engines were back.

"Maybe you're right, Thomas," Henry puffed. "Maybe I *do* have lucky trucks."

One by one, the engines returned to the shed. It was very late.

When the other engines were all asleep, Henry thought how pleased he was to have lucky trucks.

"Now I will always be on time," he puffed, happily. "And that means I can be a Really Useful Engine!"

But the next morning when Henry went to the Yard, his lucky trucks weren't there.

"Oh, no!" Henry whistled. "Where are they?"

"Edward took your trucks," puffed Thomas. "He needed them to take coal to the villages."

The Fat Controller arrived at the Yard. He had a Special for Henry. "A delivery of presents has arrived at the Airport. You must collect them and take them to the children in the villages!"

So Henry set off for the Airport. But he soon ran into trouble . . .

Gordon's Hill was very icy. Every time Henry tried to puff up the hill . . . he slid back down again. It took a long time to reach the top.

"I need my lucky trucks back!" Henry huffed. "I can't make my deliveries without them!"

Henry was worried. "I must find Edward! I must find Edward!" he puffed.

Henry steamed on through the snow. Up ahead, he saw logs across the track. They had fallen off James' flat truck and were blocking Henry's way.

"Oh, no!" puffed Henry. "If I'd had my lucky trucks, this would never have happened!"

"Where are all the presents?" snorted James. "Your Special is to go to the Airport!"

"Edward has my lucky trucks," whistled Henry. "I must find him first."

Henry shivered sadly on the track, until Rocky the rescue crane arrived.

"Don't worry," called Rocky, cheerily. "I'll have the line cleared in no time."

Soon, Rocky had cleared the logs from the track and Henry chuffed on to find Edward and his lucky trucks.

But everywhere that Henry chuffed, there were more delays.

"Sorry!" puffed Thomas. "It has taken me a long time to clear the snow from the line."

"It's not your fault," Henry wheeshed. "I need to find Edward and my lucky trucks."

And Henry puffed sadly away. He couldn't find Edward anywhere.

"I'll never see my lucky trucks again," he sighed.

But when he reached the frosty forest . . . there was Edward, with Henry's lucky trucks!

"I've found you!" Henry chuffed, excitedly.

But Henry was going too quickly. His wheels slid on the icy tracks . . . and he biffed straight into his lucky trucks!

"Oh, no! I've broken my lucky trucks!" moaned Henry, sadly.

Henry put on his brakes and wheeshed through his whistle. "I'm not going anywhere without my lucky trucks!" he huffed.

"But they're broken!" chuffed Edward. "And if you don't collect the presents soon, the children won't have anything to open!"

Henry thought about how sad the children would be. "I have to get to the Airport somehow!" he puffed. "With or without my lucky trucks!"

So, Henry set off. The tracks were still very icy and Henry's wheels started to spin and slip but he kept going.

The more Henry thought about the children, the less he thought about his lucky trucks.

Before long, Henry arrived at the Airport and his crew loaded up the presents. Then Henry steamed quickly away to start his deliveries.

"I must deliver the presents on time," he puffed. He didn't want to let the children down.

Henry puffed all over the Island, dropping off the presents. Soon, he was on his last delivery.

He steamed into the station and saw the children waiting on the platform. "Good old Henry!" they cheered.

Henry felt very proud. "I've delivered all the presents without my lucky trucks!" he peeped. "Maybe the trucks weren't so lucky, after all!"

And when Henry looked at the children's smiling faces . . . he knew he was still the luckiest engine on Sodor!

Two Great Offers for Thomas Fans!

THOMAS & FRIENDS

In every Thomas Story Library book like this one, you will find a special token. Collect the tokens and claim exclusive Thomas goodies:

Offer 1

Collect 6 tokens and we'll send you a **poster** and a **bookmark** for only **£1.**
(to cover P&P)

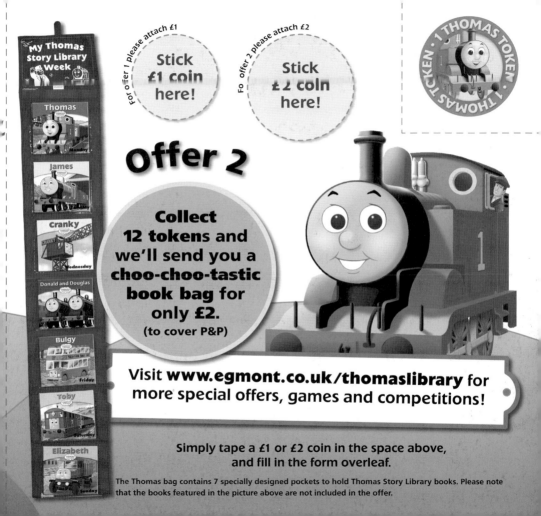

Reply Card for Thomas Goodies!

1 Yes, please send me a **Thomas poster and bookmark.**
I have enclosed **6 tokens plus a £1 coin** to cover P&P. ☐

2 Yes, please send me a **Thomas book bag.**
I have enclosed **12 tokens plus £2** to cover P&P. ☐

Simply fill in your details below and send them to:
Thomas Offers, PO BOX 715, Horsham, RH12 5WG

Fan's Name: ....

Address: ....

....

.... Date of Birth: ....

Email: ....

Name of parent/guardian: ....

Signature of parent/guardian: ....

Please allow 28 days for delivery. Offer is only available while stocks last. We reserve the right
to change the terms of this offer at any time and we offer a 14 day money back guarantee.
This does not affect your statutory rights. Offer applies to UK only. The cost applies to Postage
and Packaging (P&P).

We may occasionally wish to send you information about other Egmont children's books but if
you would rather we didn't please tick here ☐